The LOVE *Club*

DONNA FAULKNER SCHULTE

authorHOUSE®

AuthorHouse™
1663 Liberty Drive
Bloomington, IN 47403
www.authorhouse.com
Phone: 1 (800) 839-8640

Published by AuthorHouse 02/25/2016

ISBN: 978-1-5049-7564-3 (sc)
ISBN: 978-1-5049-7563-6 (e)

Print information available on the last page.

CONTENTS

Dedicated the loving memory of my father

Reese Albert Faulkner

Thanks to all my family and friends that gave me their love, support and encouragement. I love you and God bless you all.

PREFACE

Twins Mariah and Miranda are just starting their first year of High School. They are all excited and have been instructed to by their Jr. High counselor to join clubs so it would look good on their transcripts for college.

They hope their first day is going to be fun and they'll find the right club and make new friends. But as they approach the school they notice a man sitting at the edge of the woods licking the last crumb from a cracker wrapper like it was pure gold.

This breaks their heart to see someone that is that hungry and they can't get it out of their minds. As they go through the day they try to think of a solution to this problem and look for a club that may do some good in the community. It turns out to be a fruitless search.

They decide to pack food for this man and give it to him the next day as they pass. This all changes when they approach the school and see there are more people there now and they don't have enough food for all of them.

With the help of their friend Ebony they find that they can petition to start a new club. They just need to meet the right people and get things going.

See the adventures the twins have meeting new friends and starting something that will change not only their lives but the lives of many. Meet all their new friends and see as they have some of their firsts happen in their private lives. Join the first year of Mariah, Miranda and The Love Club.

CHAPTER 1

STARTING HIGH SCHOOL

It was a new day and not just any day. It was the first day of high school. The twins were trying to pick out just the right outfit that would just (WOW) everyone. They giggled as they thought of how they were going to fool everyone that didn't know them. They were identical and even family members could not tell them apart.

They brushed their long red hair and tried to decide if they should wear it braided or just let it down. They decided to let it down. Everyone always commented on their beautiful long curly red hair, and always asked them where they got their perm at. They loved saying it was natural.

They were always the center of attention where ever they went because people would look at them and ask their mom "how do you tell them apart?"

Their mom Sandy would just laugh and tell people that sometimes she had trouble too. So they pretty much got used to the attention since they were very young, which was good because it made them very outgoing.

Both girls were known for their sense of humor that sometimes got them in trouble. But overall they were really good kids and made great grades in school.

Mariah said "she wanted to be a pediatrician when she grew up" and Miranda said "she was going to be a doctor or a teacher, she hadn't decided yet. But if she became a doctor she wanted to be one that didn't have to see blood."

They had a lot of friends and they were popular at their other school but, this was high school that was a big change. Mariah said "don't worry it can't be that much difference," even when everyone said it was a big difference. She just had a positive attitude and was not going to worry about it.

She wished Miranda would just look at it like she did and stop caring if people liked her or not. Miranda was the worrier of the two.

They finally decided what to wear and got all their stuff together and ran downstairs for breakfast. Their mom got lunches together as they ate and ask them "if they wanted a ride to school?" Mariah said" no we want to walk to school today it's so nice outside. Besides you have to hurry or you're going to be late for work."

So they gave mom a hug and went on their way to school. They saw people from their school last year hanging out bus windows to yell hi to them as they walked. Mariah looked at Miranda and said "see I told you we didn't have anything to worry about, all our friends will be there too. We will not be alone with people we don't know. And we will make new friends. So let's go make it a great year."

Miranda smiled and said "as long as you are there I'll be ok. I just hope we get a lot of classes together. They had not been allowed to be in the same class before, the guidance counselor said they would learn more if they were separated. This however did not set well with the twins.

They couldn't wait for lunch so they could see each other. They had been that way since birth they had to be touching or they would cry. So they slept in one crib and still slept in one bed even though they had separate rooms.

"Remember what the guidance counselor said Mariah." Miranda said. "What did the guidance counselor say? I don't remember anything but school is getting out and we were going to Kansas."

They had been chosen by the Mayor Pro Tem Miss Simmons to go to Kansas and compete for All American City. They were going to fly on a plane for the first time in their life. They were excited and afraid.

Mariah was more afraid, because Miranda kept saying "I read about another plane crash today, I sure hope we don't get one that crashes." Then she would walk off giggling like crazy because she got to put a scare in her sister. It went like that every day one picking on the other one.

They didn't need any friends because they were each other's BFF.

They were going to Kansas with the mayor, fire chief, police chief, Miss Simmons and the 82nd Airborne band as well as a lot of other important people.

They were representing the people of Fayetteville to compete for the title of All American City. It was a great honor to win this title.

You would have thought that the people in Kansas had never seen twins before. The photographers kept taking pictures of them like no one else was there. They made the front page of the paper every day. They were beginning to feel like movie stars. It was annoying, but at the same time it was pretty cool.

"Well, said Mariah she said that we should join as many clubs as we could, because it would look good when we apply to colleges. So we need to check out all of them and find some that are fun but look impressive."

"Well as long as we are in the same ones then I have no problem with that. Miranda said. Nothing is going to ruin our first year.

I just simply won't allow it. "Mariah giggled and they walked on smiling, thinking of how great this year was going to be and the fun they were going to have.

Everything was looking good until they came up closer to the school and saw a man sitting on a log at the edge of the woods next to the school. You could tell the man was homeless by the way he was dressed. But what caught their eye the most was the fact that he had a cracker wrapper in his hand and he was licking the crumbs off like he was starving. This tore through their hearts as they saw this up close.

They had seen it in movies and on TV but never in person. Miranda said "we should help him, but what?" Mariah said "well we could give him part of our lunch and we could just share today." But when they looked at the man they were afraid to approach him.

They went through the first couple of classes, trying to find out what was going on at the school, so they would know what was popular and what was not. Then they went to lunch. "I can't even think about eating Mariah said." "I know said Miranda I couldn't stop thinking of that poor man and how we should have done something."

They went through the rest of the day in a daze. The image of that man trying to get the last crumb kept playing over and over in their head. "We can't just ignore this Mariah said, we have to do something."

"Well we can ask mom when we get home I'm sure she will have a great idea." Miranda said. That made them feel a little better, so off they went to check out clubs.

The hunt for clubs was turning out to be a big disappointment. The ones that they checked on so far were so lame, and that word was not in their vocabulary. "On to the next club," Miranda said." So off they went to check out what they had to offer.

The final bell rang and they still hadn't found anything that they were interested in. "We can just take the list home and let mom look at it and try again tomorrow." Miranda said and they walked home, but they both noticed that the log was vacant now.

They came up in the yard just as their mom was pulling in the driveway. They waved and ran to the car to help their mom unload her stuff and their baby brother CJ. They called him that because he was named after his dad whose name was Christopher Michael but every one called him Chris. He was out of town a lot because he was head of public relations for a big company that had offices all over the world.

They had a great relationship with their parents, which was unusual for teens their age. Once they were in the house their mom asked "how did school go today?" It was fine until we got at the school this morning" Mariah said. "Why what happened?" her mom asked looking a little disturbed. She knew it would take something pretty serious for them to be in a down mood the first day of school.

"Ok. What happened that took those pretty smiles off your faces? Was someone mean to you? Where the older kids bullying you? Sandy asked.

"No mom, everything went fine at school. It was what happened on the way to school that bummed us out. Miranda said. We just saw a man sitting in the woods licking a cracker wrapper and you could tell he was so hungry, but we didn't know if we should offer him half our lunch or would he be insulted."

"Well Miranda, you remember what Miss Shawana said at youth service about always be willing to put your hand out to offer help to someone in need? If they take your help you both feel better, and if they don't you know that you at least tried." Sandy said.

"Well tomorrow we'll make an extra lunch and give it to him when we pass him," Mariah said. "Yeah we can make him a really nice lunch with fruit, sandwiches and some bottled water." Miranda said. They were getting excited just thinking about helping someone. So they went into the kitchen to plan the menu for their surprise lunch, giggling all the while as usual. Sandy was glad to see her girls back to normal. She hated to see them down.

After supper they were playing with CJ and they remembered they still had a problem they needed mom's advice about, what clubs they should look into. But most important which clubs they needed to impress a college admissions office.

They decided one problem at a time and went to make a grand lunch for the homeless man. They wanted to make sure that he had enough that he might have some left over for later.

As they were getting the stuff to make sandwiches and trying to decide what kind of fruit to put in the bag Mariah said "just think if we carry him a lunch everyday he will at least be fed for 9 months, maybe by then he will find a job and everything will go better for him." "I know, Miranda said and we'll know that we had a part in it even if no one else knows, we will. I think that is why we saw him, because it was meant for us to help him. You know Miss Shawana says that God sends people into your life sometimes for a reason, maybe this is the person sent to us."

They made up the lunch and by the time they helped clean up after supper they were ready to go to bed.

As they laid down and closed their eyes they felt a warm feeling of satisfaction and peace rolled down them like a warm cuddly blanket.

They could not hardly wait for tomorrow to come. It was going to be a day they would remember for the rest of their lives. The day they could tell their kids about one day.

When they went to sleep they had smiles on their faces. Yes, they were proud of themselves. But most of all they showed mom that they were growing up to be the caring person she wanted them to be.

CHAPTER 2

A PLAN GOES WRONG

Mariah and Miranda jumped out of bed the next morning before the alarm clock went off. They could not contain their excitement. It oozed out of every pore of their being.

"Today is the day we do something really important with our lives Miranda, Mariah said. Yes, something that we can be truly proud of without anyone but us knowing we did it. This just make me feel so good inside I don't think anyone could make me feel bad.

"I know I dreamed about it last night and it all went down just like we planned it and the man was really happy Mariah, I mean really happy and it felt so good to see him smile.

I hope that is how it really goes today. Please tell me that's how it's going to go." Miranda said.

"Well of course it's going to go right, look who's doing it. Mariah said with a laugh. Have you ever known us to fail?" She was getting tickled at herself because she knew that this got to Miranda when she was trying to be serious. We are gingers and everyone knows that gingers rule. We are the ginger and she snaps her fingers." That was their little call sign.

"Stop it Mariah, I'm being serious. Why do you always do that?" Miranda said. "Because I can said, Mariah, because I can." "You are ugly; do you know that? I mean really ugly."

"Can't you take a joke? Mariah said, and if I'm ugly you are too, because we look just alike remember. Duh!" Miranda tried not to laugh.

She wanted to keep her mad face on for just a little longer so it didn't look like Mariah won the fight.

But she could feel her lips going up. "You just make me sick she said with a laugh." Then they got the giggles as they always did. They would look at each other and just start laughing again. "I don't like you Mariah, I just want you to know that." Miranda said smiling.

About the time the door opened and their mom said

"What is so funny and what has the two of you up before the alarm? I usually have to drag you out of bed."

Miranda said "Mom remember what today is? It's the day we help that man. I dreamed about it last night and everyone was so happy."

"Well I hope that is the way it works out. This is a very kind thing you're doing and I am so proud of both of you girls. Now get dressed and come on down for breakfast." Sandy said as she went to get CJ up and feed him.

The girls didn't hardly taste what they had for breakfast because they wanted to leave early to make sure they had time before school to talk to this man.

They hurried down the street giddy with anticipation.

But as they got closer to the school they were hoping what they saw was a group of students. "Please let that be students." Miranda said.

But as they got closer their hearts fell in their chest.

Standing by the log with the man were 5 other people that looked just as hungry and in need of help as he did.

"We don't have enough to feed all these people.

Miranda said almost in tears. How can there be this many people without homes and hungry?"

Mariah said "Are you for real! Don't you watch TV?

They show this on the news all the time. It's just we never saw it around here. I heard dad say the other day that he was lucky to have a job, because so many of his friends had been laid off and were having a hard time finding jobs. We are just seeing reality and it is not pretty." Mariah was trying to be the strong because she knew this meant so much to Miranda, but she was just as disappointed as Miranda was.

They passed by without looking over because they didn't want the people standing around the log to see their face and mistake it for disgust or anything negative.

When they got into the school they just weren't feeling it. "I feel so bad that we can go get food anytime we want it and if we don't want it we throw it away Miranda said. Those people would probably give anything just to be able to get one meal a day. There has got to be something that we can do to help all these people. We have to put our thinking caps on and come up with something to do that will help a lot of people not just three or four. I think we can come up with something I really do."

Mariah looked at her and said "I love your enthusiasm, and the fact that you have that much faith in us but we are just two people."

"No we are the ginger and she snapped her fingers. We can do anything if we put our minds to it. I know that we can help.

Please just promise me that you won't give up. Pleeeeeeeeeeeease." Miranda begged.

"Ok if you promise me that you will quit that whining."

Mariah said trying to look like she was aggravated, and not doing too good at it.

They went around that day and studied really hard on what clubs to join. It was mandatory that you joined at least one, if you didn't pick the school picked one for you. No one wanted that to happen. A year was a long time to be in something you were not really liking. That is what they guessed prison was like, and that would make the year drag by like it was forever.

They were walking down the hall and they saw Miss Shawana's daughter Ebony she was president of the junior class, student advisor for underclassmen. She was a wonderful girl and a great friend. Like her mother she was a Christian and could tell you anything you wanted to know out of the bible. She was the type of girl that every mother wanted their child to have for a friend and a role model.

Ebony saw the twins and ran up to them and raised her arms and said "where is my hug from my favorite twins?" Both the girls hugged her back because they loved her like a sister. Then Mariah said" Ebony did you have trouble finding which club to join when first started here?"

Ebony said" when I got here they didn't have that many clubs to choose from so I really had a hard time finding a club that I was interested in, and didn't go against my beliefs."

"What did you do? Miranda said, I mean because now they have like 40 clubs to choose from. How did that happen?"

Ebony smiled that sweet smile she was famous for and said "first you go to the guidance counselor's office and present her with your idea for the club that you think people would be interested in. If she thinks it has potential, she'll present it to the principle.

If the principle approves, you get called into the guidance office and you have 2 weeks to get 25 members to sign up for it. If you do. Then the club is officially a school club from then on." Ebony smiled and added "it's that easy".

Mariah said" easy, you call that easy? That sounds like a lot of work to me. I mean we are just freshmen we don't even know that many people, and the ones we do know wouldn't be interested in what we are."

CHAPTER 3

EBONY HELPS GET A PLAN GOING

Ebony could see that the girls had something really important that they had on their mind and that it was something that meant a lot to them. So she knew there was only one thing she could do and that was to help them.

Ebony said" Mariah and Miranda I have to go to class now but I'll give you a call when I get home, and we'll come up with something. So don't worry we got this, love you." With that she gave each one a hug and waved bye as she ran off to class.

The girls knew that something was going to happen now, because Ebony was not one to let you down. If she said that she was going to do something you could consider it done.

The twins went on the rest of the day with a great feeling that something big was about to come, and it would be great.

When the girls got home that afternoon they could not wait to tell their mom what was happening. It was all they could talk about all night. It became the whole dinner conversation.

"Well I'm very proud of you girls. Said their dad. Who knows you might get so many people that want to help out that you could make a big difference in a lot of lives. I really am proud of how caring you are about others that are less fortunate."

This really made the girls smile. Having your dad tell you he is proud of you is something really big to a girl. Their dad didn't know that this made them more determined to make this happen now. They went to do their homework, hoping to hear the phone ring, and get things started.

True to her word around 7pm Ebony called. She said "I talked to mom and she thinks that it's a great idea. She called Miss Rosa the guidance counselor, and we have a meeting with her tomorrow during our free class. So hopefully we will get all the answers we need then, and we can get the club started. Now we have to come up with a name for it. See you in the morning. Love you both."

"We love you too Ebony. Both girls said at the same time."

"Oh Miranda this is really going to happen! Mariah said so excited. I don't even know if I'll be able to sleep I'm so happy."

"Well you better not keep me up if you can't. Miranda said with a big smile. I'm excited too, but I'll just have happy dreams while I sleep." With that she threw her pillow at Mariah and fell back on her bed, ready to start dreaming.

The next morning, they hurried to get ready, like if they got to school earlier that it would make the time go by faster. It did just the opposite. They thought free period would never come.

When the bell finally rang for them to change class and it was free period, they almost had to hold each other back so they would not run down the hall and get in trouble. Ebony was already there when they got to Miss Rosa's office. "Let's get this ball rolling" Mariah said. And last night I was thinking of a name for our club. How do you like The Love Club? Because we are doing it out of love."

Everyone thought that was the perfect name. "The Love Club it is then Ebony said."

Once they were inside the waiting area of the office, all three girls were getting more excited just thinking this was really going to happen. They waited holding hands and smiling for Miss Rosa to tell them to come on in. It couldn't happen quick enough for them.

Finally, the door opened and they were lead in to sit at a big table. "Hello Ebony, Miss Rosa said. I guess this is Mariah and Miranda here?" She said as she went and shook their hand. "I have heard a lot about you two, but not that you were identical. How am I going to be able to tell you apart?

I know let me get name tags so you can't fool me." She said smiling. "I've heard a little about your plan, and I must say I am very intrigued. How did you girls come up with this idea?"

Mariah went first. "Well Miss Rosa, we saw this man in the woods beside the school and he was so hungry he licked the crumbs of the wrapper of crackers like it was going to fill him up. It would have broken your heart. So we brought extra food the next day so he could have some, but there were at least five more people with him. We couldn't give him the food because we didn't have enough for everyone. So we were trying to think of a way we could get enough food together to feed a lot more people."

"Yeah, Miranda said. That is when we asked Ebony what we could do to change this and maybe add a new club that did some good for people while we were at it."

"Well that is very commendable of all of you. Not to mention a very unselfish and kind act. Miss Rosa said. Ebony told you what you need to start a new club right? You need at least 25 people to sign a new club petition and a name for your club. Then you write a brief description of what the club is about and bring it to me. I will then present it to the principle, and I see no problem with this going through."

Mariah looked at Miranda and Ebony and smiled real big then asked." Do you think we will have any trouble getting 25 people who want to join our club?"

"No we'll talk to the most popular kids in school and with them backing us we will probably have so many sign up we have to turn people away" Ebony said. "I know just who to go to first too."

"Then we better get to signing up people now so we can get this club started before the end of the year." Mariah said.

"I'm so excited said Miranda, I just know this is going to work and people will be willing to join. So let's get this baby Rolling".

"Each of us make a list of people we know that have a lot of pull around school and talk to them. Then have them get some of their friends involved and that will be a great start." said Ebony.

So off they all went to make list of the people that they needed to get on their side. By tomorrow they would be able to start reeling people in. It was good to feel like this was going to be done and not just an idea.

They all went home and composed a list of people they thought would best help them. "I sure hope these people are as interested in making a difference as we are." Mariah said.

Miranda looked at her and said "don't we hang around with great people?" "Well yes Mariah said, we have the best friends anyone could ask for. But that doesn't mean they would want to get involved in this."

"You have to have faith Mariah, I believe that God wants us to do this and you know as well as I do if you have God on your team everything is possible. Good night and sweet dreams my beautiful sister. Love you."

"Good night to you too, my sweet sister. I'm so lucky to have you for my sister." Mariah said.

After a little more chatter, the two talked their selves to sleep. They dreamed of nothing but how well all this would be when they got it started. It was a wonderful dream and oh how they hoped it was going to be just like that in real life.

Mariah and Miranda woke up the next morning with a burst of energy. "Today we make a dent in our plan." Mariah says.

When they got to school they noticed more people in the Camp in the woods. "Where are all these people coming from?" Miranda asked.

"The news said that a lot of people were losing their jobs, and that was causing them to lose their homes also Mariah said.

Mom said that she and Daddy were lucky that they still had their jobs. She said they were lucky that they worked in a field that people needed. I hope she is right."

"Well then we must make it up to those who are not as lucky. We have to get this going faster. Because the crowd is getting bigger. Did you see those little children there? They weren't much bigger than CJ. Can you imagine him out there?" Miranda said as she shuddered at just the thought of having to live like that. She couldn't even stand thinking about it without feeling sad.

They stepped in the front hallway just as Ebony came up. She had a stake of papers in her hand and her smile only meant one thing. GOOD NEWS!

With her were four girls that Miranda and Mariah did not know. That only meant one thing Ebony had started recruitment and it was going to work out perfect.

CHAPTER 4

PLANS START HAPPENING

When they got to Ebony she said" ladies I would like to introduce you to Emily she is the Captain of the varsity cheerleading squad, Jennifer and Devin they are in charge of junior varsity cheerleading teams. This is Aniya she is Captain of the female soccer team. Ladies this is Mariah and Miranda. They are the geniuses that thought up The Love Club. So let's make it real."

"Well said Emily as I look around I see a lot of smart women. You know what that means, don't you? With smart women with determination. Anything is possible. So I don't see a problem, I see a circle of solutions. We have this ladies."

Devin being a cheerleader threw her arms up and legs out cheering "let's go get them." Aniya said" she only speaks cheerleading, but don't worry I'll translate for you." Devin's face turned red and they all had a good laugh and knew it was the beginning of a new friendship. A bond with four new friends that would end up lasting for life.

Emily was blonde with blue eyes just like you expect every cheerleader to be and very pretty. Her smile was infectious.

Jennifer and Devin had long dark hair and were both very pretty. They too were very friendly and not stuck up. Aniya had very long black hair. She looked like an island princess. The twins tried to imagine her kicking around in the dirt. It was hard. The twins were not used to girls like this not acting like they were so much better than everyone. In Jr. High girls like that snubbed everyone but their little followers. High School was looking to be a lot better.

Devin said" I have just one question for you two. How are we supposed to tell you apart? Because I've been staring the whole time and it's like seeing double. We have to do something to be able to tell which one is which."

Ebony laughed and said" I can't tell them apart and I have known them since they were born. I just say ok which one are you today." Because they had been known to change classes sometimes for a gag, just to see how long or if the teacher would catch on at all.

Miranda said "we have school ID badges but, they messed up so we each have 2 badges with both our names on them. But when we get around you we'll put the right badge on. We promise not to fool you." Then smiled.

Aniya said" how come I don't feel completely at ease with that smile? You two look like you would love to play jokes on people."

Mariah said" well yes we do play tricks on people, but you are now our friends so you are exempt. You get a free ticket. Like a get out of jail free card, you could say."

They all laughed and knew they would be great friends. It felt like they had known each other forever.

The bell rang and Devin said" Ok let's meet up at lunch and see how far we are with the signatures, and what else we can do to speed this up to get these people fed." So off they all went to go to class feeling pretty good about everything. It was like they were destined to meet and be good friends. God's plan was surely working.

In Miranda's first class she ran into her new friend Jennifer who was in her class for CNA. They both wanted to get into the medical field so they took all the health care classes, so they could leave school with a CNA certificate when they graduated.

This would let them get college credit during High School. Mariah was doing it too but she didn't get to be in class with them.

Miranda went up to Jennifer and said" Can I talk to you a second?" Jennifer said" sure we'll partner up and that way we can talk while we practice on the dummy."

"Oh yeah Miranda said who did they get to volunteer today?" They both just giggled and went and stood by a bed waiting for instructions.

Once they had their dummy on the bed they were allowed to talk to each other, but until then they had to stand tall and wait quietly until given instructions. They stood there trying to keep a straight face, but they were having a really hard time because they both got a case of giggles from the joke.

Miranda said "Do you think we will have any trouble getting people interested in our club for real?" Jennifer said" No way girl. Emily, Devin and Aniya were talking to me and we already came up with a way to get some food bank started for the club once it is approved. We are going to talk to our coach Mrs. Jernigan and Aniya's mom Miss Sam who is the gym teacher and soccer coach, and see if we can't have people to get a discount on their ticket if they bring in food items that has a pull top or noodles that can be cooked over a fire.

Maybe nutrition bars or stuff that can be eaten without cooking. But we have a lot of other ideas and when we get all our heads together I'm sure we can come up with plenty of really good plans that can help these people."

Miranda smiled and said "I'm so glad we met such caring people. I guess we better get to saving this one here before she dies. It would be terrible to lose our first patient because we were talking." They both giggled and started working on their CPR doll. Trying to save her life for a good grade.

They both knew CPR they just wanted to get certified so they could get on to the next college course credit, with this program they would start college with courses already added to their college transcript which would allow them to skip a lot of courses they really didn't need. It was a good idea, and they were glad they had someone who cared enough to advise them of this.

Everything was going great, they couldn't wait to see what the next day would bring. But right now it was perfect.

CHAPTER 5

NEW HELP ARRIVES

After what seemed to be the longest day they had ever had, Mariah and Miranda finally met up in the hall so they could walk to their lockers and get their stuff together to go home.

While they were at their lockers up walked Emily, Devin and Aniya and four of the cutest guys the twins had seen at the school. They started trying to comb their hair with their fingers and stand in a stance that looked like they hadn't even noticed the guys. But they had noticed, boy had they noticed.

Jennifer came walking down the hall at the same time in a fast manner so she could get there before everyone started talking, but at the same time trying not to run. She got there just as Emily was about to introduce the guys to Mariah and Miranda. Then she looked around and said" hey where is Ebony? Shouldn't she be here too?

Emily said" she had to leave to help her mother set up for bible study tonight at the church. But she wanted to make sure that I introduced our newest recruits to the girls."

Mariah was thinking well come on and introduce them because she already had her eyes on one of them and she wanted to make sure she knew everything there was to know about him.

Emily said" Mariah and Miranda I would like you to meet Al he is the student body president of the whole school.

Then we have Jaylin and Chris they are our defensive line backers for the varsity football team, and just happen to be the captain and co-captain of the team. They lead us to the finals last year and we won the championship. Then this tall drink of water is David he is the captain of the varsity basketball team. Boys these are the twins we were telling you about that wanted to get The Love Club started.

Al started the conversation with the girls. He said" As student body president first let me welcome you to our school and if you have any problems with anything or anyone just tell me and I'll put my body guards here on it." Then he pointed to the big football players behind him.

Then Chris said" you wish we were your body guards as much crap as you talk." Then they all started laughing except the twins, they didn't get it because they didn't know what the story was behind Al being student body president.

Jaylin looked at the twins and saw the confused look on their faces, and smiled the prettiest smile Mariah had ever seen on a guy. She just kept staring at his beautiful blue eyes and he had her full attention.

So Jaylin said" let me tell you what is so funny about this guy needing body guards." The twins were giving them their full attention but not as much a Mariah. She was hanging on his every word.

Jaylin said" Al is the cut up of our school. He keeps everyone in stitches and is sometimes known to take some really dumb dares. Well last year when it came time to vote for officers for this year some guys dared Al to run for student body president and he had to give a really off the wall speech that promised stuff that no one could possibly do. He took the dare, and told them no problem he would do it and then they would have to wash his car for a month if he didn't chicken out."

"Well Jaylin continued." "Speech day came and every one that was running for office was on stage to give their speeches. Student body president was the last group. There were four students running for that position besides Al. We sat there and listened to everyone talk about how they would improve teacher student relations, make the lunches better and the same stuff everybody always promises when they want to be elected. Then came Al's turn. He promised a drink machine beside the door of every class room. He would have freshmen run in the rooms' right before lunch and see if any upper classmen wanted to order take out, and that they would get it before lunch so when we came out of class they would have it waiting for us still hot. Then he promised to have junior and senior relaxation days two times a week. That is where you could come to school in your pajamas and slippers and just put your feet up on the desk in front of you and relax all day.

But the biggest, craziest promise was that if you were not good in a subject then you could get the brains to do your homework, and give you the answers to the test so you would not flunk and your high school transcripts would look great."

Chris giggled and said" Then they announced that he won. The four that were running ask for a recount and a couple of the girls were crying, but he won by a long shot."

Al said" I don't think anyone was as surprised as I was. I thought it was the guys who dared me trying to play a joke. When I found out it was real I looked them up and gave them a schedule for when they could wash my car. So I guess you could say it was a win for me. But of course they wouldn't let me keep any of my campaign promises. But enough about me let's talk about this club you want to start. Emily and Devin told us about some of it and I like it, I really do."

David said" I like it because when I went to New York this summer on vacation you couldn't walk down the street without seeing homeless people. My dad gave some of them money but that only solved the problem temporarily. We need to come up with something that is going to last and help more than just a few people."

Al was tall and had blondish brown hair and had been smiling since the first second they saw him. Jaylin and Chris had dark hair. Chris had hazel eyes that just cut through you and Jaylin had the bluest eyes they had seen a guy have. David have blondish brown hair and blue eyes and was like all the guys very tall and all of them very good looking. Not one of them acted stuck up like they did at their old school. Yeah they were going to like High School a lot.

Well then Mariah said" Miranda and I don't have anything planned for tomorrow. We could all meet at our house and hang out at the pool and make some plans. Maybe even have a little cookout.

But it wouldn't be right to have a meeting without Ebony because she has been with us from the start on this. So why don't we all exchange phone numbers and we can call each other and see if tomorrow is ok. If that is alright with everyone, that is?"

Everyone exchanged numbers and said their goodbyes and off they went to go home or what they had planned for the afternoon.

Miranda was smiling and giggling all way to the bus. This was getting on Mariah's nerves because she knew Miranda was about to let her have it about something and she was enjoying way too much.

"Alright smarty pants I know you are about to bust with something so spit it out" Mariah said. Miranda laughed and said" I just like the cool way you got that boy Jaylin's phone number and have him agree to come over to the house so we could discuss it by the pool.

That was pretty clever I have to give props on that little play. "All the while she kept giggling.

"I have you know I was only thinking of the club and trying to get it started for your information Miranda said Mariah. I didn't even notice those guys like that. I was just interested in what they were saying to see if they could help us with the club."

"Sure you were Mariah, Miranda said. Sure you were. You think I didn't notice they were hunks too?"

Mariah said" So you weren't looking at anyone in particular? You didn't pick not one of them that you were going to pay special attention to?"

"Well for your information I certainly did. As a matter of a fact I pick him out as soon as I laid eyes on him. Now you can guess which one I picked. Miranda said."

"Let's see. Mariah said knowing your taste in guys you are always looking at the big athletic type. But they have to have a cute face to go with that body. So let me figure this out. Wait you aren't liking Jaylin too are you?"

Miranda laughed and said" I saw the way you were drooling over him. So no I wouldn't even look at him. Plus, I know that Devin likes David and Al has a girlfriend. That leaves only one which is Chris. He is such a hunk; how could you not notice him.

Mariah said "Yeah he is good looking, but there was something about Jaylin's eye that just drew me in. But enough talk about boys and let us keep our minds on the task at hand. We'll worry about the boys after we get the ball rolling on our club."

They asked their mother if they could have it like a pool party with a cook out so they could have fun as well as having a meeting too.

When she said yes and went to the store they set out getting everything set up, but in a way where it looked like it had not been set up. Especially the seating. They set that up just right.

CHAPTER 6

THE FIRST MEETING

Well just as everyone promised they called and set up to meet at Mariah and Miranda's house. They had everything set up and all the snacks in bowls waiting for everyone to start arriving.

"This is going to be a blast said Miranda. The only problem we have is to make sure we keep our minds on the club and keep a clear view of what our goals are. Then we'll study on getting the guys."

They both laughed and set up everything anxiously waiting for the arrival of their new friends. They went upstairs and picked out which bathing suit and cover up they were going to wear. It had to be just the right one. Cute but not showing too much and something that would definitely catch the eyes of the boys.

Mariah finally picked her hot pink one, while Miranda picked her purple one. Then they tied the long scarf around their waist so it added the just right touch to set off the outfit.

Then they braided each other's hair, looked in the mirror gave each other a high five. "Let's go downstairs now and help mom finish up the food. Said Miranda, so everything will be ready when they come and we won't be running around while everyone is trying to talk."

They had just finished setting the last plate on the patio table when the doorbell rang. Ebony was the first to arrive which was no surprise to the girls. She always came early to any event to see if she could help out. She was all about helping others and that is why everyone liked being around her. She had a heart of gold and never let anything interfere with her belief in God.

She was well respected for that alone, because she let it be known right off the bat. She was real and if you didn't want to know the truth, then she was not the one to ask. If you ask her, you got the truth even if it was not what you wanted to hear. You could not have a better friend.

"Well aren't we dressed cute today Ebony said with a smile? Would this have anything to do with any certain people that are coming to this meeting?"

Mariah said" Oh no we just got these so we wanted to wear them so mom wouldn't think we didn't like them. But if a certain someone likes it then this will become my favorite bathing suit ever." That got all the girls laughing and they started laying stuff out for the cook out.

"Just out of curiosity Mariah said. Is Jaylin, you know like involved with anyone? Or maybe likes someone not like a friend?

Not that it matters that much. I was just curious. because I don't want to take him away from his personal life to much if he does. You know what I mean don't you?"

"Oh yeah, we know exactly what you mean giggled Miranda. You're about as subtle as an H bomb." She looked at Ebony and said "someone has it bad, really bad. Don't you think?"

Ebony still laughing said" Well what are you dressed up for Miranda? Are you just trying to make your mom happy too?"

"Oh I was just wearing mine so Mariah wouldn't look so conspicuous, you know what I'm talking about don't you?"

"Yeah I know exactly what you're talking about, and his name is Chris, Ebony said, and his favorite color just happens to be purple like his jersey."

"Oh really? Said Miranda I did not know this. Thank you for telling me now I know to tell my mother to buy me everything in purple."

All the girls were laughing when the doorbell rang. "Oh my goodness said Mariah how do I look? Is my hair alright? Somebody else get the door."

Ebony went to answer the door and came back smiling. "Mariah you can calm down, it's Miranda that needs to be nervous, because it's Chris."

Miranda said" Well how do I look? Is my hair ok? Hang on let me sit here and act like I don't notice him."

Chris walked in looking as good as Miranda had remembered and waved at everyone. "How are all you girls doing today? He said.

"Well we are just doing fine Miranda said. Are you by yourself? You could have brought your girlfriend with you if you wanted to." Chris grinned and said "I would have but I don't have one."

"Oh that is a shame. Said Miranda I would have never thought that you didn't have someone special because you are so nice."

Mariah leaned over and whispered. "Oh that was real subtle Miranda, about as subtle as a building falling on his head."

Miranda gave Mariah that I'll get you later look, and let out a nervous laugh. "Well Chris you can sit over here and tell me about yourself. I bet you have such an interesting life."

Ebony and Mariah went inside because they didn't want Chris to catch them laughing and think they were laughing at him. But they just loved watching Miranda squirm and boy was she squirming.

But then the doorbell rang again and they looked at each other. Mariah said "I wonder if it my time to squirm?" But it was Devin and Emily. Mariah let out a sigh and tried to get ready for when it would be Jaylin at the door. She didn't want to appear nervous at all. "Just keep cool as a cucumber Mariah" she said to herself, just be cool as a cucumber."

That was easier said than done as the doorbell rang again. This time it was Jaylin and Mariah could feel her heart beating through her skin. She straightened her clothes and went to answer the door. Thinking all the way of something cleaver to say when she opened the door.

Well as it turned out she didn't have to think too hard. As soon as she opened the door to let Jaylin in her flip flop caught the edge of the entrance rug corner, and she literally fell into his arms.

It was hard to tell which was the reddest her hair or her face. Ebony, Devin, Emily and Chris just stood there with a total look of shock on their face. But Miranda was on the floor laughing so hard she could hardly breathe. All the while trying to say "I'm so sorry but that was funny."

Jaylin said" I've always wanted to have a girl fall for me. I'm sure glad it was one as pretty as you." Mariah smiled and said "right now I just want to crawl in a hole and hide." "Why asked Jaylin? Now we have broken the ice and we can start getting to know each other better. I was going to use today as a way to find out about you anyway. So let's just start over."

So Jaylin put his hand out and said "Hi, my name is Jaylin and I am very pleased to meet you." Mariah took his hand and said "Mariah and I'm pleased to meet you too. I hope I didn't hurt anything when I fell on you."

When everyone else saw that all the tension had been broken and no one was hurt they all started laughing too. All except Miranda she was still laughing from before. Like they always said "You're my sister and I love you but you fall and I am going to laugh at you." That was something they both held very true to. It didn't matter where they were or which one fell the other one would lose it, and laugh uncontrollable.

Finally, when they got Miranda under control and Mariah had thrown those shoes as far away from her as possible they went and started munching by the pool waiting for everyone else to arrive.

The phone rang and it was Aniya "she asked if it would be possible if she brought someone with her that was new to the school? She thought she would be a good addition to the group, but she would also have to bring her baby brother with her. Her name was Lila and her mom had just gotten a job so she had to watch her baby brother till her mom got off."

Miranda said" sure the more the merrier and her little brother could play with their little brother C.J. If her mom didn't care. Hang one second and let me ask, Ok? Mom said it's a go, see all of you in a few. Mom said ask your mom if she wants come in for coffee." Aniya said "she would." and hung up.

When Miranda told everyone about the new girl they all couldn't wait to meet her. In the meantime, Al and his girlfriend Megan who was a photographer for the school paper and annual. She also worked freestyle selling pictures to the town paper. She planned to be a big time photographer when she got out of college.

That is all she had wanted to be since she was little and got her very first camera for Christmas. This year she was going to get the top of the line camera just like the professionals had.

Megan was Interested in everything that going on around her. She wanted to have it down on photograph for the future generations to see how things used to be. When Al had told her about the club she jumped in with both feet, not once hesitating. Anything to make a difference. That is what Al liked about her was that she really cared and didn't just talk about it, she did everything she could to do something about it.

The doorbell rang again. When Mariah opened the door this time everyone stood up and clapped. Her face turned beet red, and you could tell she had a few choice words she wanted to say to everyone, but she just smiled and bowed saying "thank you, thank you. I'll be here 7 days a week. I can't say that about some others but I will be here."

Then she looked at Miranda because deep inside she knew who thought that little performance up. Just a hunch, but she was willing to bet on it.

It was David at the door and he wasn't alone. He said" I'm sorry I should have called but I lost your number but I was closer to your house than mine, but if it's too much?" "No Miranda said come on in we'd love to meet your friends."

David said "Everyone this is Patience but everyone calls her Pay Pay and this is Buddy. She plays girls basketball and Buddy is on the team with me he's my co-captain and my main man on the court. They would like to join the club if you don't mind?

"Well of course not Mariah said come on in and meet the crowd and strange person that we let sit with us so she doesn't hurt herself. You might want to sit far away from her she has something really wrong with her. I think she's from another planet or something.

David introduce everyone and I'll start bringing out some drinks and food with her. Come on You."

Miranda couldn't stop giggling she knew she had gotten Mariah good because she was trying everything she could to come up with something to get her back with and failing so bad. So she thought she would fold and say sorry.

"Mariah I feel really bad I got everybody to clap and embarrass you, will you please forgive me my beautiful sister, please?" But she just couldn't keep a straight face while she was saying it. This made Mariah even madder.

"How can you say you're sorry and laugh at the same time? That tells me you don't mean it. I will get you back before the day is over. You just wait it is going to be a good one too. Don't you think for one minute that I'm going to forget. I'm not." She just kept saying this as she was getting cups and plates together.

Miranda just kept giggling. She kept thinking to herself is it sick that I'm enjoy this just too much? Oh well, might as well enjoy it while I can just in case she does think of something good to even the score.

CHAPTER 7

A SURPRISE NEW MEMBER

Just as they were coming out of the kitchen the doorbell rang again. This time it was Aniya and when she walked in and the girl Lila was with her with her baby brother.

Miranda recognized the baby at once, then Mariah caught on. It was the little baby by the fire. Lila looked down at the floor and shyly said "hello."

Mariah and Miranda took her hand and said "we don't allow anyone to be shy around here. You step in that door you become family. So come on and meet everyone. Lila smiled she felt at ease almost immediately. Something she hadn't felt in a long time.

Sandy came out and said" let me see that baby. Aren't you just the cutest thing? You want to go play with C.J. and have some lunch? Lila was so surprised he didn't even cry he just smiled and giggled.

"His name is Nicky, Lila said." "Well hello Nicky, Sandy said playing with his little fingers and how old are you?" Lila said He's 10 months old. I can't believe it; he usually doesn't go to strangers. He must sense that you are a nice lady."

"Well you are both welcome here anytime that you want to come over Lila and if you need anything you don't see just yell." Sandy said. Aniya's Mom Samantha had already called and explained Lila's situation, but she had not had a chance to tip the girl off before she got back from the store. When she got home the house was full and she didn't want to discuss it where someone else might hear by accident.

Lila's mom, Lila and her baby brother were homeless till last week. They found room for them at the women's shelter, plus a temp job that was working at night. Since it was at night Samantha, Aniya's mom said they would keep the baby so she would have daycare and could work. They met her because she started going to their church. Everyone wanted to help her get back on her feet. It was a wonderful church they believed we are all brothers and sisters and Jesus wants us to look out for each other. This is one thing they did too. No one went away without help.

When they all went in where everyone else were at, Mariah saw David was sitting where she was supposed to be sitting. All the girls were in their group and the boys in their group. This had to be broken up at once. But how?

The twins went into the kitchen to get some more stuff when their mother pulled them in the den behind the door. She explained everything and told them to watch their mouth so that they didn't say anything to hurt Lila's feelings.

Going in the kitchen they were whispering to each other "I told you I saw that little boy somewhere." Mariah looked up saw Lila and froze. "Lila I'm so sorry. It doesn't matter you are still welcome here. We just hate you had to go through this. Please forgive us for talking about it."

Lila said" You don't need to apologize. When I found out what you two were doing for people you never met. People that you could just pass by if you wanted to, but didn't. You're trying to start a club to help. I wanted to meet you. So I know anything that you say is not in hate or jest. It was just concern. I wanted say thank you and ask how can I help?"

Miranda, Mariah and Lila all grabbed each other with tears in their eyes and hugged each other like they didn't want to ever let go. Then they heard Aniya saying "Wait your giving out hugs and didn't call me, move over." They broke loose and laughed. Lila said well nice moment while it lasted."

Miranda said "Well you don't have to worry we won't say a word. No one will ever hear it out of our mouth."

Lila said" No they'll hear it out of mine. I lived it so I know what it feels like. What they need. What food are the most helpful to them that they can cook over a fire and is easy to carry around and open. So please let me tell of our experience. That is the problem. People that have never been through it don't know what it takes to survive out there.

If I hadn't been there I would have done like everyone else and brought canned goods. But what if it's not a pop top? What if you feeding more than one person? If you have a small child, they can't drink from a hot can. I made a list if you don't mind?"

"Not at all Mariah said you are a genius. Plus, may I say you are also my new hero."

They started setting the table, their mom started bringing out pizzas and nachos. The guys started cheering Sandy for the food. She took a bow and said "thank you, thank you. There is more coming." Then the doorbell rang. "Please excuse me, I shall return." She left the room followed by cheers.

It was Jennifer she had a part time job and so she got there just as the food was being served. When she walked onto the patio Devin said" yay Jennifer made in time for lunch. Yay, Yay.

Aniya looked at Lila and said "She is 100% cheerleader. We don't know what she is going to do when she gets out of high school and college, unless she gets on a professional team. Then I have no idea as she gets to old for that. Lord help us." Without even blinking Devin said "I'll coach." Everyone lost it.

'Ok let's pray. Ebony would you lead us Miranda said?"

The boys acted like they had not ate in ages and Lila put very little on her plate. Mariah had to excuse herself from the table.

Mariah's mom found her in the upstairs bathroom with tears in her eyes, and ask her "what was wrong?"

"Mom we have so much food that they are playing with it in front of Lila who no telling how many nights had to go to bed hungry. Yet she is putting so little on her plate like she is afraid someone will not get any. It just breaks my heart someone would have to live like that. We have to make this work even more now than ever before, People in the greatest country in the world! Children living in the woods not eating. It has to stop and it has to stop with this generation."

Sandy hugged her daughter and said "I wish I could shield you from all this terrible stuff, but I can't. What we can do is exactly what you're doing. Try to change the things that we can change and make a difference where we can. Now wipe your eyes because the last thing Lila wants is your pity.

She is a brave girl go give her your strength." She kissed her on the forehead and sent her downstairs.

When she got down stairs everyone looked at her and saw her eyes were red and asked "What was the matter?"

Miranda who had figured it out said "I guess I put a little too much hot sauce on the end of your taco. Sorrrrrrrrry."

Everyone laughed. Mariah looked at her sister with a thank you, I love you look, and said "I told you I'm going to get you and I mean it. So just keep it up it'll just get worse."

Miranda said "I said I'm sorry. Gee." Everyone just kept laughing.

After food and swimming they all sat down and started talking business. Miranda handed out note books and put them where she wanted everyone to sit. Just so happened Chris ended up right next to her and Jaylin ended up next to Mariah. Ebony leaned over and said" Funny how that worked out isn't it?"

Miranda said "Ebony you just say a prayer he notices me and quit picking on me. You got a cute boyfriend can't I have one too? I've been good."

Ebony Laughed and said" I'll put in a word with Big Man and Chris too, how about that?"

Miranda Said "I knew you were my BFF for a reason. Love you." Then they called the meeting to order.

Mariah said "Before anything is said tonight I want to introduce you to one of the bravest people I've met in a long time. She would like to speak to us before we start talking about things to do. I can honestly say I think we need to listen to her, because I think she can be classified as an expert in this field. So I now turn the floor over to Lila. Let's please give her a big hand."

Devin stood up "Yay Lila who's the best Lila, Lila, yes, yes, yes." Aniya said" That means she likes you."

Lila stood up and said "Thank you but I'm not the hero here. The heroes are the ones that are trying to help people just because they want to help out of the kindness of their heart. I want to help because until last week that was me." Everyone that didn't know dropped their jaw and tried not to stare.

"I know you've seen me at school so you didn't know, but that was because I would go clean up in the gym before school started and the janitor let us wash our clothes in the gym washers. Then we met Aniya's mom and started going to her church and got us a room in women's center, got my mom a job and even helps by babysitting. God is good. Soon we will be able to find a place and start living life again. We used to live like this. Then one day my Dad went to work and got in a wreck. He didn't make it and didn't have enough insurance. It can happen to anyone at any time without warning, and your life as you know it is over. I was so afraid someone would see me at night there and then when I went to class act like I had some kind of disease or something.

I don't know how I would have acted if it had happened to someone before me. I hope that I would have been as loving and caring as all of you, but I don't know. I might have been one of the people who shunned someone like me. You can't look at a person and always tell what kind of problems they are having. It is not a position I would wish on anyone."

Every one of the girls had tears running down their faces. They couldn't imagine their fathers not coming home one night but to lose everything at once too. That was just too much, and she was still so positive. They wondered could they be that strong if it was them.

Lila said" I didn't come here for your pity. But when I found out that you were trying to get a club together for the homeless and hungry I wanted to help. There are things they need that no one thinks about. So I made a list of stuff that would really be helpful to them. These I know 1st hand. Thank you. It has been an honor meeting all of you."

She turned to go and everyone yelled "hey where you going?"

Lila said "I didn't want to bust in on your group. I just wanted to say what I had to say."

Chris stood up and said "sit down little lady. Your part of this group for life now the only way to get out is die." They laughed and Devin yelled "group hug"

The lifelong friends were growing bigger every day, and they would be friends for life.

CHAPTER 8

THE BOYS SURPRISE THE GIRLS

Chris said "Since I'm already standing then I guess I'll go ahead and give my speech. You girls said you needed 25 names to put on your petition to get the club started, well here is the name of every guy on the football, basketball, baseball, wrestling and soccer team. I'd say you more than made it over your required amount to petition for your club."

"Now for the great news. You all know that the Coach Drake is also our woodshop teacher, right? Well every year we build a house and we auction it off. Jaylin show them that paper.

Jaylin pulled out a paper where a man had made little mini shelters that would fit in a parking space and had a fold down bed, drawers and a handle that pulled like a wagon. Chris said "The coach said we could build as many as we could with the wood we have for the house. We would use all that and then if we can raise money to buy more we can build more.

The people that live by the river could really use them because they have no shelter at all. That's what I have to report I'll turn the floor over to Jaylin now."

Jaylin stood up and "said I've got a list of friends who also signed to petition for the club. I also talked to my mom about it, and she said that if we got it going that she would get her ladies group to help out in any way we needed help. Like bake sales to raise money. Yard sales, Dinners. That could be the money we need for the little shelters. Thank you." Then he kept bowing and waving till Chris grabbed his waist and said "Sit your goofy butt down."

David, Buddy and Pay Pay stood up and said "We had the idea of having a girl vs boy basketball game all the money would go to the club except what is made in the food stand. We talked to the coaches they said if the club passes they would approve of it.

Al stood up and said "My uncle works for the paper so he said anything that we do for this he'll cover it and put it in the paper. This might bring in money from other charities or private citizens."

The girls were speechless. The boys had just taken everything under control and left very little for them to even have to worry about. They had really expected to have to push the boys to get them to do anything, instead they did it all.

Miranda said "We are so proud of you guys. You basically did it all by yourself. Usually guys don't show an interest they just say they'll help and then when you need them they make themselves scarce.

But not you guys you stepped up said you would and did exactly that. Thank you for taking us seriously."

Chris said "I have a friend and his brother is on drugs and homeless. Sometimes we ride by to check on him and I see these people. I give them what money I have but it is not enough for all of them. When I heard what you were doing all I could think was this is my chance to really make a difference and I wasn't going to miss out. So I thank you girls for coming in and starting something like this. Kind of like a kick in the pants we've been needing in the club dept. for years. All we needed were a couple of redheads."

Miranda said "You better watch it Chris you walking on thin ice there."

"Ok, Ok Chris said One thing my dad taught me never get a Redhead mad at you. He said it could be dangerous to your health."

Miranda said "Your dad gave you some good advice you might want to follow it."

Chris said "That's it guys we need to sit and listen now for our safety. My dad always said never stop a woman from having her say or you will pay for it the rest of your life." Everyone laughed.

"No but to be serious for a second Chris said. We have had some great ideas thrown out here today and I think everyone has done a great job. I really think that this is going to be something big and I'm glad to be a part of it."

Jaylin stood up and said "I agree with Chris 100% on this. Plus, the fact we have met some pretty great people because of this great idea. That I think was a big plus, I would like to say thank you all for allowing me to be a part of this." He then sat down so Aniya could talk.

Aniya stood up and said "I have another friend named Randi. She couldn't come tonight but she is on the school dance group. When I told her about it she said that she was definitely interested. She is going to bring it up to her dance group and see how many of them want to get involved." Everyone that we have talked to really wants to help. Like Chris said we just needed someone to get the whole thing in the works. For this Mariah and Miranda, we raise our cups to you. Thank you for your good hearts and sharing your great idea with all of us so we can help in something that needs to be taken care of, I just hope that our generation is the one that can end it.

That is my wish. Let this end with our generation.

No American should have to live like that. We are the greatest country in the world. We should not have this going on in these days." With that she sat down and teared up again just knowing what Lila and her family had gone through broke her heart.

Everyone gave her a standing ovation. Yelling "way to go Aniya. Well said." They all knew that this was something they were going to fight to make it go away. They were willing to give all their extra time and energy for this worthy cause.

CHAPTER 9

PLAN IS READY FOR APPROVAL

Aniya got up and said "She had talked to her mom and as the soccer coach she had the idea that if you brought in 2 food items you would get in the game two dollars off. Thanks to Lila we now have a list that you can pick from to bring."

Mariah and Miranda and Ebony stood up and Ebony said "This meeting turned out better than we could have ever dreamed of. The only thing that can stop us now is if they vote against us and I can't see any reason that they would do that because it would bring honor to our school since Al is going to have it covered by the paper. Megan is going to be taking pictures for the school paper and the annual.

Now enough meeting for today let's have some fun and go swimming. Lila went and sat at the side by herself, so Mariah went to see what the problem was. "I don't have a swim suit" she said. "You do now, come on girl. We told you, your one of us now you'll never go without again." Mariah said.

Lila got a suit and they had the best day ever. Especially when Chris swam over to Miranda and they hung on the side of the pool talking for what seemed like forever. Then she looked over and saw Mariah had Jaylin's full attention. This had been a perfect day. Surely God planned this day himself because it was to perfect.

Everyone stayed till about 8 P.M. and everyone was in a great mood. Sandy got to meet Lila's mom and they got along great. She said "They were hiring where she worked and she would talk to someone for her.

The pay was really good and she would have insurance and she also might be able to help her get a house." It seemed like everything was falling into place. All because of The Love Club and it hadn't even started yet. The twins took this as a great sign, and they believed God sent you signs with all their heart.

Lila came over to them and said "I just want to thank you so much for what you're doing and making me feel so welcome today. It is one of the best days any of us have had in a long time. I felt like a normal person today. I haven't had that feeling in a while."

Mariah and Miranda both hugged her tight and Mariah said "You are one of us and will always be. We don't pick our friends by where they live or the clothes they wear. We pick them by how they treat others and how they act towards us. You have a great personality and you didn't have to get up there tonight and tell all that about yourself, but you did.

Not for pity or what you could get out of it, but to help others. That is what we look for in a friend and you showed it all in one swift move what kind of person you were. So Lila we would be honored if you would be our friend."

All of them had tears in their eyes as they hugged each other. But it was a hug that they would treasure for life. Because it was the start of a lifetime relationship. Lila became more like a sister than a friend. A sister that they didn't have to look at and see themselves. Something they always wanted, was a sister that was different looking who would give them a biased opinion.

This is something that twins could not do because if they thought it looked good on the other one they didn't want them to know so they could wear different clothes sometimes and be individuals. So many times the twins would have the same outfit just in their favorite color if they had it.

It was cute dressing alike when they were young, but now they wanted to be different since they had gotten older. So it required telling the other one that the outfit was terrible so they wouldn't want to copy it.

As they thought of their clothes they ask Lila to come in their room and see if there was anything that she wanted while she was there. That would give their moms time to talk and they could play dress up.

It had turned out to be a great day. Everything has worked out perfect, and everyone had learned a good lesson. You can't judge people just by looking at them. A smile can hide a terrible secret. They had seen Lila in the halls but never once would they have guessed the horrible life she was going to have to go to. While they looked at the clock and couldn't wait to leave, Lila probably prayed the bell would not ring because she knew where she had to go.

Mariah told Miranda and her Mom" I will never judge another person again. Nor will I take all the people and things we have for granted. I just can't even stand to think what she must have gone through on top of losing her dad. Then to lose everything else right after that. Then to have a baby in the mix also. It just breaks my heart. Thank God that those days are over for them. It just makes me more determined to get this club going so we can have the same ending for a lot more people. Oh yeah, and if I haven't said it today I love all of you with all my heart. Get used to hearing it, because I also learned you never know when it will be the last time." Then she hugged all of them like it was the last time she would ever get to hug them.

When their dad came home late that night they both rushed him and hugged him so hard he grunted in pain. "To what do I owe all this he said to the twins?"

"Just wanted you know how much we loved you dad." They both chimed in together. Goodnight dad we love you so much." With one last kiss they went off to bed.

He looked up at Sandy and said "Need I ask?"

Sandy told him "Just enjoy it our girls learned how privileged they were today.

I'm so proud of them. They really are good kids, even when they are torturing each other to death." They both laughed, hugged and went up to bed. It had been an interesting day that was for sure.

CHAPTER 10

THE BIG MEETING IS SET

Miranda, Mariah and Ebony sat outside the Counselors office. Miss Rosa and the principle Mrs. Faulkner had set aside an hour for them to present their ideas. The girls were hoping some of the others would make it in time to join the meeting and help them out. They were so nervous. It was one thing to talk to each other about this but now they were going to have to present this in front of the highest ranking adults at the school and that gave them butterflies in their stomach.

When the door opened up they sat up in their chair and waited for the adults. But to their surprise it was everyone including some faces that they had not even seen before.

Along with the kids Miss Shawana and Aniya's mom Sam with Coach Drake and the dance teacher Mrs. Fletcher. Once they heard about the meeting they wanted to show the kids they supported them.

Finally, the door opened and in came Mrs. Faulkner and Miss Rosa into the meeting room. They both looked surprised to see the crowd. They had only expected 3 teen girls. This really impressed both of them.

"Well I see you came armed and ready. said Miss Rosa. Looks like you did your homework. I must tell you I am very impressed at the people you have picked to support your cause. It shows real leader skills."

We aren't trying to be leaders Miss Rosa. Miranda said. We just want to get people that care and will actually make a difference. We owe Ebony all the credit for picking out who we should get on our team. She is the one that picked the people that would have the most influence on the other students."

Ebony said "I can't take credit for these people having good hearts and willing to give their time and energy to help other. I thank God all of these people wanted to help. It makes you feel a lot better about the world when you can get this many people involved in such a short time. But Mariah and Miranda deserve all the credit, because they are the ones that saw there was a problem and we could help solve it."

Mrs. Faulkner said "Well I think it speaks volumes for all of you. I am so proud to have such wonderful young adults representing this school.

As you know my husband was one that helped everyone all his life and I am a firm believer in reaching out and helping those who need a helping hand. Sometimes life throws you a curve ball and you just have to do the best you can do with what you got. No one ever knows when it can happen to them.

Unfortunately, these days we see it happening more often than we would like to see. I vote yes without hesitation. What about you Miss Rosa?

Miss Rosa said "I also am proud of each and every one of you. You show great maturity and a great sense of compassion for your fellow man with this club. Coach Drake and Coach Sam said they would be the club staff sponsors, so I will also vote yes."

Everyone started clapping and hugging each other.

"We did it Ebony. Mariah said. We did it." Then she stopped and looked at Mrs. Faulkner and Miss Rosa and asked "when can we start doing some of our projects?"

Mrs. Faulkner laughed and said "whenever your Staff sponsors say you can. If you want to have a meeting today and it is alright with them for you to use their classroom, then by all means start as soon as you want. Again I want to tell each of you I'm so proud of you. When you turned your plans into Miss Rosa for your club and she gave them to me. I really was expecting just a couple of ideas and something just to take up time. I could not believe all the great ideas you had already come up with and hadn't even started the club yet. So as of this moment we have a new club on our list. What did you say the name of it was going to be?"

Mariah said "We decided on The Love Club if that is alright with you Mrs. Faulkner?"

Mrs. Faulkner smiled and said "I think that would be the perfect name for this club. Oh and Coach Drake if you come by my house I have a lot of lumber that was left over when I was having some remodeling done.

You and your club are more than welcome to all of it as well as the nails that go with it. Congratulations to all you members of The Love Club. I know I will be hearing great things about you."

Megan said "Let's get our first picture of The Love Club for the paper and the annual. Mrs. Faulkner and Miss Rosa would you do us the honor of posing with us, since you are here for the beginning?

Mrs. Faulkner and Miss Rosa both smiled and at the same time said "We would be honored to." They looked at each other and laughed as they got in the group to pose for the picture.

The Love Club was officially a Club now so with it being in the paper they were hoping to get all kinds of new members. The more people they had the more people they could help. This was the greatest day of all their school days ever in their whole life. The twins could not stop smiling. Nothing could ruin this year now.

CHAPTER 11

THE CLUB GOES INTO ACTION

As soon as the meeting was over they all ran out into the school yard cheering and screaming. They were so happy. All their ideas had been accepted and they were going to make a difference. This made all of them feel like they were really winners.

Sam said "Well boys and girls why don't we go to my class and let's start putting some of these ideas into action. I already got permission for the food drive for Tuesday's soccer game. But I had another idea I'd like to run by you if you don't mind?"

The group looked at her and Mariah said "Why would we care? I have a strange feeling that you and Coach Drake had already gone to bat for us before we went in there today. Because that went by too easy."

Coach Drake said "We just told them we had some wonderful kids that were trying to make a big difference in the world, and we were lucky enough to have them at our school. We also thought this would make our school look good. Mrs. Faulkner is for anything that helps someone. Especially if it makes the school look good. So no we didn't do it. Your ideas did it. You kids get all the credit and I'm thankful that you are allowing me to be included in it."

Al said "Well Megan and I have to be somewhere before five o'clock today so we will get up with you tomorrow to find out what was said at the meeting. We wouldn't normally miss the first meeting but this is really important. So we'll see you all later. Great work guys.

As student body president I am very pleased to say that this is a major thing that happened here today and I also am glad you let me be a part of this school history." With that he left with Megan.

"Wonder what those two have to do that is more important than our first meeting?" Ebony said

Jaylin said "Well as bad as he wanted this club I'm willing to bet that it has something to do with the club. That's how Al is, full of surprises. No telling what that mind of his has come up with. But I'm sure it is something spectacular."

"Well I hope it's better than his speech. David said.

Everyone laughed and they all headed to the classroom for The Love Clubs first official meeting.

They could not contain their excitement. You could feel it in the air all the positive energy coming from this crowd was something wonderful to behold.

CHAPTER 12

THE FIRST OFFICIAL CLUB MEETING

They all took a seat as they got to the classroom.

Sam said "First order of business is to elect club officers. Do I have any nominations for President of the club?"

Ebony held her hand up. "Yes Ebony, who would you like to nominate?" Sam said.

"Well I know this is unusual, but I nominate both Mariah and Miranda since all this was their baby to start with. They act like one person anyway." She laughed

Sam said "Does anyone want to second that? Everyone raised their hands. "So we have a power pair as presidents.

Congratulations girls do you accept the nomination.

I think we know how everyone else feels about it." She giggled.

"On behave of my sister and myself said Miranda. We would be honored and thank you for your confidence in us. Then she said I would like to nominate Ebony for treasurer if she wouldn't mind doing that."

Sam said "How does everyone feel about that?"

It was met with a loud applause. "So Ebony do you accept this nomination?"

"I too would be honored Said Ebony. At this time, I would also like to nominate Megan as secretary. I think she would be great for the job since she wants to do the pictures and put us in the school paper. She would already be taking notes for that, so we could, as they say kill two birds with one stone."

Sam said "I agree with you about that makes perfect sense. Do we have any trouble with this nomination?"

As expected no one had a problem with this nomination. So the club was really official now with officers and all. It was great.

Mariah said "Since Megan is not here at the moment I'll take notes for her and give them to her tomorrow along with the news that she is the new secretary."

Finally, everything decided Sam said "I would like to run this idea by all of you. We talked about people paying with food to get into the games? Well I was thinking what about having a food gift card drive.

This way they can get a hot meal while they are moving around. Plus, if it is raining they can't build a fire to cook on. With gift cards they could go into a warm building and eat a hot meal. So what do you guys think of this idea?"

Chris said "I think that is a great Idea. With a five-dollar coupon and some change you can get a whole large pizza at those pizza restaurants that are all over town.

There is practically a fast food place at every corner. I know if it was me I would much rather have pizza or burgers than canned goods to eat."

Sam said "Well yes Chris, I think everyone would rather have fast food. But I'm not talking about instead of canned goods and packaged food. I'm thinking along with for them to have a treat sometimes."

Lila said "I know I would have loved for someone to give us gift cards when we were living in the car. It would have made us feel normal for a little while. That is one thing you miss the most when you are out there. So yes gift cards are a great idea."

"Mariah write that down. We will come up with a plan to get a lot of gift cards to hand out." Sam said.

Coach Drake looked at his watch and said "Well I think our first meeting went very well.

We are going to start tomorrow on one of those pull trailers in wood shop. I'm going online tonight and see if I can get hold of the guy that came up with the idea. He put his site in the paper for people to contact him. First I'll make sure he is alright with us copying his idea then if he has a blue print or something to kind of lead us through it. So all of you be careful getting home and we'll see you in the morning."

Miranda said "Great meeting and with that I pronounce this meeting dismissed. Thank you all for coming and all of your ideas and support."

Everyone got their stuff together and started out.

Chris stopped the girls and said "Do you pretty ladies want me to give you a ride home? I'm going right by your house on the way home."

Miranda tried to hide her excitement. "That would be so nice of you Chris. Are you sure it's no trouble?"

Jaylin came walking up and said "Of course it is no trouble. Since when is driving pretty girls home a problem? We'll be the lucky ones everyone getting to see us with two pretty red heads."

Chris said "You can quit laying it on so thick Jaylin. They already said they would ride with us. Boy I was afraid he was going to scare you off he was laying it on so thick."

Mariah laughed and said "Hey no problem. Sometimes a girl likes a guy to lay it on a little thick.

Makes us feel good and then it also gives us power."

Jaylin said "What do you mean it gives you power?

Mariah said "Because you let the girl know how much you like her and she can hold it over your head."

Jaylin said "For real girls do that? I mean you wouldn't do that to a guy would you? You do know I just joke around a lot right. I'm not really like that."

Mariah laughed and said "I was just messing with you. Girls can do that too you know. I know you are a nice guy and would never disrespect a girl or use her for arm candy. You're too good for that. That is why we feel comfortable with you and Chris."

They started off and Chris said "Will you just keep quite Jaylin before you dig a hole you can't get out of and mess things up for me. Because Miranda I would like to ask you to the movies this weekend if you would like to go?"

Miranda thought her heart was going to come out of her shirt. "I would love to Chris. I'll ask my mom to make sure it's alright, but for now the answer is yes."

Jaylin said "Well Mariah what about it you want to make it a double date? Mariah wanted to scream it out that yes she wanted to go, but she held it in. In a calm cool voice, she said "That would be wonderful Jaylin.

They pulled up to their house and the girls got out of the car and said their good-byes. They waved the boys off as they pulled away and went down the road. Then they totally lost it. They grabbed each other's shoulders and jumped up and down squealing like little kids. Then they skipped to the front door singing "we have a date, we have a date."

They didn't care if it was mature or not. Today had been a perfect day from morning to now. All because of The Love Club. Yes, that was a perfect name for the club, just perfect.

Miranda just about ran over Mariah in the house to get to their mother and ask her if they could go.

It would kill them if she said no. But it was just a movie. Plus, they would be together. That is what they would use to plead their case.

Their mom was nowhere to be found. She must have had to work late or stopped somewhere on the way home. It was torture till they heard her car in the yard. Then they rushed her as she came in the door carrying C.J. in her arms.

"What is it girls Sandy said? You act like you haven't seen me in years. How did everything go today?

"That is what we wanted to talk to you about Miranda said. We got approved for the club and we got asked out for the movies this weekend. I know you don't want us dating yet but Mom it's Chris and Jaylin. It would be a double date so it would really be just like friends going to the movies. What do you say mom can we go? Can we?"

"Slow down a minute Sandy said I just got in the house good. Let me lay your brother down and then we can talk." It seemed like it took her forever to lay C.J. down. Then she came back in the kitchen where the girls were eagerly awaiting her decision.

She sat down at the table with the twins and said "So tell me about how the club thing went?" The girls just stared at her. Really was she just going to ignore that they told her two of the cutest most popular boys in school asked them out to them movies? Or was she just messing with them to see if she could get a rise out of them? Whatever it was it wasn't funny.

Sandy decided that they had suffered enough and she smiled at them and said "I know I said I wanted to wait till you were more mature to start dating. So we will take into consideration that because of your birthday you had to start school a year later than everyone else, which means you will soon be old enough to date.

Plus, the fact that what you girls have accomplished in just the little time you have been in high school. I think that you have shown me that you are mature and can make good decisions. With all these factors together I think that I can say yes and not have second thoughts about it. I'm very proud of both of you. So call them and tell them you can go."

Then she had two girls around her neck so tight she thought they were going to chock her. She was so glad that they were having a good year so far. She just hoped it stayed that way. Then again she was kind of sad that it meant her babies were growing up and would soon be grown and gone. I just won't think of that now she thought to herself. I will keep them with me as long as possible.

"We love you Mom. Mariah said as they ran up to their room to call the boys. This was going to be the best year. It couldn't possibly get any better. That's what they though anyway. Boy did they have a surprise coming.

CHAPTER 13

AN EVEN BIGGER SURPRISE

The next morning, they got up and made sure that they looked really nice. Hair had to be perfect and just the right outfits. Then they went downstairs for breakfast.

"Well there are my two celebrities, their Dad said.

Seems you made the front page of the paper with your new school club. Quite a big article to go with it too." Then he turned the paper around and sure enough there it was the picture that Megan had taken in the meeting room when the club was approved. So that is where Al and Megan went yesterday. They had to get there before the press closed down. Al had said he had family at the paper.

They sat at the table and read the article. It was good and they were sure that this would probably help the club with donations and help.

"Well now we know why he was voted president, Mariah said. It's because he knows how to get things done and how to get publicity on things that needed to be noticed."

The biggest surprise came when they got to school.

Kids where getting off the buses and out of cars and they had bags with what looked like groceries in them. The club had just started and already it was making a difference.

Ebony, Emily, Jennifer and Devin ran up to them as soon as they saw them. Ebony said "Did you see what is happening? One article in the paper and just go look in the meeting room."

Everyone followed her to the school meeting room and sure enough the table, chairs and floor was filled with bags of food some blankets and packs of toilet paper. Just like the list that was in the paper.

Sam came walking in behind them and said "Well I can't believe my eyes. This town is so great. Just let them know what you need and there it is. What do you say we meet this afternoon and make some gift bags up for those people next to the school today?

Then later we'll make some and carry them around to where there are other groups. Does that sound like a plan?"

"That sounds great Mariah said. We'll be getting more tomorrow at the soccer game and then Friday at the football game. If people keep donating like this maybe, we can end this problem for real."

"Well it's a start said Emily. Once you start something that is the biggest step right there.

The rest is just bound to fall into place. This is just so wonderful. I'm so glad you thought of it Mariah and Miranda. Thanks for letting me be a part of it."

"What? Miranda said. We should be thanking all of you guys for helping us get this thing off and running. Without all of you we would not have gotten the signatures or the right people behind it to get others interested. There is no one person that is responsible for this. The Love Club did it and a club is more than one person. It is a lot of people working together to get something done. So the thanks goes out to everyone in the club."

"Well then Emily said. To The Love Club. May we continue to have success and put a big huge bite in hunger and helping the homeless." Everyone put their hands on top of one another and said together "Go Love Club!"

That afternoon they went and got gift bags together so they could take them to the people in the woods by the school. While they were doing that Coach Drake came in and said "he had some wonderful news."

They sat down to hear him out. Also they needed to rest their backs from all the bending over from sorting things into the correct piles. They were going to have to find another place to store everything and sorting it would make it easier to carry out.

Coach Drake said "Remember when I told you I was going to get up with the guy who makes those little trailers for the homeless online? Well I did and he responded back right away. He said not only did he not mind us copying his design, but he is coming down to get us started on making them. He said he had hoped that his story would encourage other people to do it in their town. So far we were the only ones that had replied to him about doing the same, and he was tickled to death we are doing it."

Sam and everyone else that were sorting were about in tears. Not because they were unhappy, but just the opposite. Everything was falling into place just as Emily had predicted it would. Sam was especially proud of Coach Drake because they were dating and she knew if he could care that much for strangers, then he was definitely the type of man she needed in her life.

Sam's ex-husband had not been a bad man. He was just a man that didn't have time for work and a family. He could not do both so he chose work. It had been a hard time for her and Aniya when he left. If it had not of been for the good people at her church and the kindness of others she didn't know how she would have gotten through it.

Coach Drake made sure that he included Aniya in everything so she felt important and loved. For that Sam loved him. Yes, he was a good man and she was lucky to have him on their team.

After they had gotten about thirty bags together.

Coach Drake pulled his pick-up truck around so they could take some to the people next to them.

When they pulled up the people around the fire looked afraid at first. All the kids jumped out of the truck and some came walking over on foot. They walked up to the people and shook their hands and told them they had something for them. This set the people at ease.

They started handing out the bags and the smiles on the people's faces were worth every second of work they had put into it. Megan again was snapping pictures and no one seemed to mind. They were just thankful that someone was helping them. They decided just to leave all the bags there and let them divvy them out.

They noticed that these people weren't selfish they put everything together to be shared by all. Here they had nothing but yet they shared whatever they had with each other. They were like a small village the way they lived. The kids thought everyone could learn from these people. Those that had little were less selfish than those that had a lot.

After they had given all the bags out, they told the people they would be back and if they needed anything to please let them know. All the time all were trying to keep dry eyes. It really moved and humbled them being around such a situation. It should not be like this in America.

Lila knew most of the people there by name. But she even noticed that there were new ones that weren't there before. This was not a good sign. It meant the problem was getting worse. She really hoped that they could make a difference. She didn't want to see anyone like this. Because she knew firsthand how bad it could be.

They left and let the tears fall finally. It was heart-warming and heartbreaking at the same time.

Once back at the school everyone in the club moved the remaining things to the school storage building in the back behind the gym. That they decided would be the new Love Club storage shed.

Everyone was tired but in a good way and so they all could go home knowing they did something good today. That is what the club was supposed to do make people feel good about themselves while helping others. It was working just as planned.

CHAPTER 14

THE CLUB IS IN THE NEWS

The next day the pictures that Megan had taken were in the paper again with a write up telling what happened and telling about the game that night.

It was urging everyone to come out and bring gift cards to get into the game for $1.00. A five-dollar card would get them in for one dollar and a ten-dollar card would get two people in for one dollar. This was a deal considering it was seven dollars a person to get in usually.

Everyone was so excited when they all met together that morning. Chris said "We are getting to be celebrities lately. Al and Megan you wouldn't know anything about that would you?"

Al said "Hey it's my job as president to make sure this school has a good name and reputation. If it causes people to come in and want to help the club out, then that is just a perk. Plus, Megan wants to be a photographer when she gets out of school. This is giving her street credit. It's a win-win situation."

Mariah said "You're absolutely right about that. It sure helped the last time you put it in the paper. Let's hope it has a big impact on gift card night.

That would be wonderful if we got a whole pile of gift cards to give out. I can't hardly wait till tonight now to see how it plays out.

Just as they were walking into the school they noticed Coach Drake with some guy they didn't know. "I wonder if that is the trailer guy. Asked Chris."

About the time he got the words out of his mouth Coach Drake and the man came towards them.

"These are some of the kids that got the club together Mr. Walters. They brought your article into wood shop wondering if we could do that. Which lead me to you. We are quite proud of these kids. They are good kids with big hearts."

"Well I am pleased to meet all of you. I also consider it a huge compliment that you liked my idea enough to want to do the same for the homeless in your town Mr. Walters said. That was what I wanted people to do was to copy my idea, and it took a group from high school to catch up on the idea.

So I would like to thank you very much for carrying the torch on for me. Now I'll see you later. The coach and I have a trailer to build."

With that off they went to the woodshop. Chris and Jaylin followed them since they had woodshop first period. They waved at everyone and disappeared down the hallway.

"Yes it certainly looks like we are going to make a difference with this club. It really makes you feels good to be able to help people. I never thought that it could make me feel that good to help people you don't even know. "Jennifer said.

Ebony said "It always feels good to give. That's why they say it is better to give than to receive. I am just glad that we have so many people in this town that are willing to give. Those who give with a loving heart will be blessed. Just remember that when you have doubt about helping someone. All of you have a blessed day and I will see you tonight at the game."

With that she was off to her class.

Mariah and Miranda could not believe the turnout at the game that night. The gift cards were pouring in and they couldn't wait to hand these out and see the looks on the faces of people that received them.

At the end of the night they had collected over four hundred and forty cards. This was better than they ever expected. Of course Megan was there to take pictures. Everyone lined up holding handfuls of gift cards and smiling. They knew this would end up in the paper too.

The next night at the football game people were lined up with bags at the ticket booth. While Emily, Jennifer and Devin cheered. Chris and Jaylin were on the field ready to play. Miranda, Mariah, Al, Aniya, David, Pay Pay, Buddy, Lila, Ebony, Randi and all the other members of the club collected the bags with food, blankets and umbrellas into the wagons to store. Some people were still giving gift cards. It was so great it filled the hearts of all the kids.

"People really do care said Mariah. You just have to let them know that you need their help. This is beautiful."

Of course Megan was catching all of it on film.

This was going to be the feel good story of the year and she was going to have it recorded. It would look good in her portfolio later on for college. Little did she know that she was launching her career before college. All her work was being noticed by some pretty important people that would later take her to the top.

The boys came across that night too and won the game 21 to 0. So they had plenty to celebrate afterwards. Sam and Coach Drake took everyone out for pizza and they had a great time. Everyone was in the highest of spirits. Devin had a right to cheer at the pizza parlor and no one even made fun. It was a wonderful night; another night they would remember for years to come.

With all that going on Mariah and Miranda still had their minds on Saturday night and going to the movies with Chris and Jaylin. Their very first date.

This was the year for a lot of firsts.

Saturday morning came and the girls were beside themselves with what to wear and if they should wear make-up or just go natural. They decided to wear the make-up. Just to look a little different for their first date.

Sandy helped the girls straighten their hair which made it go way down their back. By the time the boys got there Mariah and Miranda looked entirely different from what Chris and Jaylin had ever seen.

When the doorbell rang Sandy opened it and let the boys come in as the girls were coming down the stairs. The look on Chris and Jaylin's face let them know they chose the right style.

"Who are these knockouts? Chris said. I don't believe we've met." Jaylin just stared with his jaw hanging.

Chris reached over and pushed Jaylin's mouth closed and said "Ok Jaylin don't be so obvious." Everyone just laughed and that broke the awkwardness of the moment.

Sandy told them to have a great time and drive careful. She stood and watched her babies stepping out as young women and a tear ran down her cheek.

She wondered where the years went so fast. Seemed just like yesterday they were so tiny in the ICU unit at the nursery. As she wiped her cheek she thought one day she would be holding their babies. Yes, her girls were growing up.

They went to see a scary movie that turned out to be more of a comedy than a horror movie. Half way through the movie Chris reached over and held Miranda's hand. It made it quite clear that they were going to be spending more time together.

Jaylin bumped Mariah's arm a couple of times but she kept her arms across her chest. She always was the stubborn one. Jaylin was satisfied with just sitting beside her and listening to her infectious laugh. He decided right then and there this was going to be the girl for him. Mariah would have no problem with this decision. None at all.

When the date was over and they stopped to get a burger the time flew by. Soon it was time to take the twins home. Now the guys had to decide if they were going to try to get a kiss tonight. The girls were hoping they would get their first kiss tonight. That was for sure.

The boys walked them to the door and Chris could not believe Jaylin beat him to it. After he had been sitting at the movies with his hands empty. Then he goes in for the kiss first. It shocked Chris and Miranda.

Chris said "Well I guess I'll see you later. I had a great time and you looked beautiful as always tonight." Miranda smiled and said "Me too, I really liked the movie." With that Chris leaned in and gave her that very first kiss. It was just the perfect first date as far as the girls were concerned. They wouldn't have changed a thing.

They went into the house and Sandy was sitting in the living room waiting for the full report. Miranda and Mariah both started talking at the same time.

Their mom said "Slow down I can't understand you when you both talk at the same time. They stayed up talking till two in the morning. Then Sandy sent them to bed because she had to get up with the baby in the morning. If not, they would have talked all night.

Sunday morning their dad said you made the paper again. Sure enough the club members were on the front page and the whole page three collecting donations and the story told all about what the kids were doing with The Love Club. Mariah and Miranda especially liked the part about how the club was doing so much good for the community.

Everyone went and got ready for church. The girls couldn't wait to see the others at church so they could talk about the news article about the club.

Ebony and her mother Shawana were waiting outside the church with a copy of the paper. Little did they know that it was going to be part of the sermon that day. Yes, they were making an impact and it felt good. This is what they wanted the club to do and it didn't let them down. The preacher said that the club was bringing the town together in a positive way. That was all they needed to hear.

Everyone sat in the pews and smiled so full of pride that they were a part of this wonderful miracle. They had never expected it to go this well, but they were sure glad it did. Then the preacher said let us all thank the Good Lord for such wonderful youth and their spirit for giving. The church members stood and clapped for the kids that were in the club. They all glowed with pride.

Chris called Miranda that afternoon and Jaylin called Mariah. Other than that it was just a regular Sunday and everyone just rested. It had been a busy week but worth every second of work.

A few weeks later they were surprised to see news vans in front of the school. They all wondered what was happening, so they ran into the crowd to see. There was Coach Drake and Mr Walters with the very first set of trailers. They were about six and half feet long and had handles so they could be pulled like a wagon to be moved from place to place. Each one had two fold down beds. They were made sturdy and thick so the people in them would be warm and dry. They were going to present the first ones to two older men because of health problems.

Coach Drake motioned for Miranda and Mariah to come over there. When they got over to where he was standing they saw everyone in the club standing with him and Mr. Walters.

The cameraman pointed the camera at the twins and the reporter said "I understand that you two are the ones that started this whole thing to start with. What gave you the idea?"

Miranda said "First off we can't take credit for The Love Club. It was a group effort and we have so many wonderful people who are giving their time and energy to make sure that it works."

Mariah said "That's right and she pointed to all the cheerleaders. They had a car wash and raised quite a bit of money for us to purchase umbrellas, rain ponchos, blankets and pillows for our cause. The guys are the ones that worked on the trailers and got those built.

Some kids cut grass to raise money to donate for the cause. In just a few weeks all these wonderful people have come together and made a big difference. The good news is that this is just the beginning we have just started. Now that the club is official this will continue to go on and a lot of people will be helped. So sir all the credit goes to all these wonderful people, not just us."

"Well the reporter said "The thing is that all of you have made a very big difference in the lives of so many people who would not have food and warmth without this wonderful club. I can't wait to see just how much you all accomplish."

Then he looked at the camera and said "So we will keep up with The Love Club and keep you updated on their progress." With that he signed out and wrapped up the interview.

The men that received the trailers were so happy. They were checking them out inside with the beds and floors. Yes, they were very happy. The coach promised the others that there would be more coming.

Again the looks on the faces of these people were worth more than money could buy. They came by each member and shook their hands and told them thank you for all their caring and help.

Each one told them God bless you as they went off with their food bags that Sam and some of the members got together while they were looking over the trailers.

That night sure enough it was all on the news. It was going to be seen all over the United States. They were going to be noticed everywhere they went.

All the kids were so excited that they were burning each other's cell phones up. It had gone crazy, but crazy good.

Miranda and Mariah both thought this is going to be the best year ever. Things were going great with the club and with Chris and Jaylin. They were on top of the world nothing could knock them down or so they thought.

CHAPTER 15

THE CLUB GETS COMPETITION

The doorbell rang and Miranda ran to see who it was.

Standing on the porch were Ebony, Emily, Jennifer, Devin, AL, Megan, Chris, Jaylin and David. "Hey guys what's up? Said Miranda.

AL said "Have you been watching the news today?

"No Miranda said. Why what's on it?

"They have another school that started a club called Caring Kids. They stole our idea and are acting like it was theirs." Miranda said "Where is this school located?" Chris said it's on the other side of town.

One of the private schools. They are totally biting off our idea. The only thing they are not doing right now is building the trailers. I guess they don't have woodshop in the ritzy schools."

Mariah said "Well now let's wait a minute. We didn't do this for fame or anything so that just means more people will be helped. But I have an idea that will really help more people. We act like we are mad. Then we ride over there and say something to them about well your club isn't all that because you aren't making trailers. I'd be willing to bet they start producing trailers within the next week. That way it won't all be on us to do, and more people will benefit from it."

Ebony looked at her and said "Mariah you are a genius. You also need to remind me not to ever make you mad at me. They all laughed and set up a time for their soon to be famous ride. The ride that would set up a dominos effect that would hit more than just their town.

They all decided to go after school on Monday.

So after their last class everyone piled into all the cars that were available and went across town.

When they got to the school they saw the news paper van. It was taking pictures of them handing out food bags to some homeless people that had come to tables they had set up in the parking lot.

Everyone got out of the cars and walked up to the tables. A snotty acting girl came over and said the line starts over there. It took everything Miranda had to keep calm then. "Hold me Back she whispered." She cleared her throat and said "We didn't come here to get anything we just came by to see if you copied us correctly. By looking around I see you stopped with the bags as to where we went on to building trailers.

The girl looked at her with pure fire in her eyes. "I'm Candice, I started this club here. We are going to start on the trailers very soon." "Good said Miranda because if you are going to copy us do it all."

With that she walked off and they all got back in the cars and drove off away from the school before they busted out laughing. It was easier than they thought it would be to get that girls goat. Now they would keep watching to see if they did make any trailers or else they would have to pay them another visit.

Sure enough a couple of weeks later front page had them presenting a trailer just like the ones the boys were making to a homeless lady. Standing with them was Mr. Walters. He had gotten his dream. People were following his idea and using it to help the homeless have a roof over their heads. He later sent them a thank you letter for spreading the word.

They couldn't imagine him thanking them when he was the one that was doing the good work. So they sent him a thank you plant and attached to it was a picture of two more people getting trailers from their school. It was so true the Lord worked in Mysterious ways.

They started noticing that more schools in different states were forming clubs like The Love Club and this made them happy. Even though they couldn't act like it did. Because with teens and high school it is all about the rivalry. Each school trying to outdo the other. But of course if they didn't think it was bothering the other school they just wouldn't try as hard. It was all about the rivalry, but in this case that was a good thing.

All through the year the kids became closer and got their pictures in the paper one week and the next week the other schools would be in there for doing more. It ended up with about 50 trailers for their school and around 75 for the other school. But their school could afford more so they expected them to do more. They didn't completely solve the homeless problem but they put a big dent in it and brought attention to it for the city council to have to take some kind of action. Homeless shelters started opening up all over town.

They liked to think that The Love Club had a hand in getting some of this done. But as long as it got done it didn't matter who did it. After all that was what the club was supposed to do was bring awareness and it certainly had done that. So they could all look back and know they did a good job and be proud of themselves.

CHAPTER 16

PROM TIME

It was funny how time goes by when you're having fun is so true. The year seemed like it was flying by.

Seemed like they had just started school and here it was a month till the end of school. Devin talked them into joining the prom decorating committee. Which they didn't mind because the school allowed you to bring someone that was in a lower grade if you were dating them. So of course Chris and Jaylin had asked them months ago.

The senior and juniors had to vote on a theme name for the prom. Emily suggested they stick with what the school had been doing all year and name it Making a Better Future. She was hoping they would vote on her name so bad.

The other names were all song themes that really had nothing to do with what the school had been doing all year, so she was pretty sure hers had a good chance of winning. Especially since the student body president was one of the ones that did the voting. She was sure he would have some pull in the name. She was sure going to make sure he knew her preference.

The girls all went together with their mom's in tow to pick out the perfect prom dress. Of course Miranda had to have purple and Mariah had to have her favorite color pink. The only problem they were going to have was that they had never wore high heels in their life. Mariah said "If I about broke my neck in flip flops, high heels are going to really kill me. I'm going to have to practice every day till prom. Because if I fall at prom just leave me on the floor to die. Don't even try to help me, because I'll just die of embarrassment."

Miranda laughed and said "Well you better be nice to me between now and then or I might just trip you."

Mariah laughed and said "I'm not worried because you can't walk in heels any better than I can. So it will just be a contest to see who falls first, and you better believe I'm betting on you." They both put on the heels they were holding and wobbled and laughed at each other till they didn't know where it was the heels or they were just too tickled to stand up. Whatever it was they weren't doing too good at it right now. So they decided they would just try later when it wasn't so funny.

They practiced everyday till both of them got actually quite good at it. Mariah said "That still stands about leaving me to die if I fall."

Miranda said "Don't you worry sis as long as I'm around I'll always have your back. I'll be there for you so you won't fall. Besides that as soon as we get in there we can kick these suckers off and go barefoot." Mariah smiled and said "That's a plan."

They couldn't hardly wait for prom night. It would be the last time they got to spend a lot of time with Al and Megan because they were seniors. They were going away to college in California so they would not be coming home often. It was going to leave a big void at the school without them. Emily was going to N.C. State so Jennifer or Devin would take her place as captain of the cheer squad. So there was going to be a void there. With all the good there would be some sad times too. But they had great memories with each of them. They would cherish those for life.

Lila was going to be with them. They had become real close friends. Lila's mom got that job with Sandy and was making good money now. They were renting a house down the street from Aniya's house. Everybody was so happy for them they threw them a house warming party and they got a lot of nice things. The house came furnished so they didn't have to worry about that, which worked out perfect.

Just like the preacher said when you do right by others good things will happen for you.

God was looking out for that family because they were kind and caring people. Lila had done a lot with the club this year. Just because she knew what it was like and didn't want others to have to go through the same thing. She was so selfless. She also met a nice boy and she was coming over to get ready for the prom with Aniya and Ebony.

The boys rented a stretch limo and all of them were going to go together in it. So to save money the girls decided to all come over to Mariah and Miranda's house and get ready so the guys wouldn't have to pay mileage to all the houses. Plus the fact they could all help each other get their make-up and hair right. They were just making it a girl's day and having a good time getting ready for their very first formal dance.

When everyone finished getting ready they didn't even look like the same girls. They all looked like beautiful princesses.

The boys were going to go crazy when they saw what their girlfriends looked like. They all stayed upstairs and waited for the boys to arrive so they could make the dramatic decent down the stairs in front of the guys to see their reactions. Mariah told everyone the same thing she told Miranda about if she fell. They all had to promise to leave her there. Of course no one would, but at least it eased the nerves with the kidding.

At seven on the nose the doorbell rang. Sandy opened the door to 5 very handsome guys. Dressed from head to toe in the very best the tux store had to offer. Each guy got their comber bun to match their girlfriends dress. Poor Jaylin was getting picked on all the way over because Mariah's dress was pink.

The other guys were lucky Ebony and Lila had Blue dresses and Miranda had a deep purple just like the jerseys. So it left Jaylin in a circle of one with a girly (as the guys kept telling him) color. But for Mariah he would put up with it for tonight, because she was that special to him.

The guys stood and waited till the first girl came to the top of the stairs. The girls flip coins to see would come down the stairs in what order. Lila was the lucky winner she got to go first. Then came Miranda down behind her, Ebony and Aniya went next. Mariah was last. They stood on the steps in order looking more like a beauty pageant than a prom. While the boys looked up at their dates with the exact looks that the girls were hoping for.

"WOW!" all the guys said at the same time. Chris was the first one to say it. "You girls look like beauty queens." All the other guys shook their head like they were saying "What he said." Each guy then went to the stairs and took the hand of their date and escorted them down the steps.

"Everybody stay where you are the twin's dad yelled out. I have to get a picture." He then proceeded to line everyone up and pose them so he could get just the right light. The girls just shook their heads and said "Parents, they will embarrass you. It is their job and ours have it down to an art." Then they heard the phrase they were hoping he would skip. "Everyone say cheese now." The twins could not stand when someone said that. They could not understand why you just couldn't say smile.

Finally, the pictures were taken and it was time to leave. They all walked out to the limo on the arm of their date. All the neighbors were looking as they lined out of the house and waving their approval.

Miranda said "You know you look good when the neighbors get in on it. So we must rock."

Chris looked at her smiled and said "You certainly do." Her night was made right then.

When they arrived at the school they got the same reaction. Everyone was staring at all of them as they got out of the limo. It was another special memory for them to file in the back of their mind for later years. For when your old and you need that one memory to brighten your day. This was going to be at the top of their list.

The night went by so fast they were having so much fun with all of their friends. Even when they had to go looking under tables because Mariah could not remember which one she took her shoes off at. They just made light of it and treated it like they were on a scavenger hunt. Mariah said "If they didn't cost so much I would leave them, but you would never see me again because my parents would kill me." They laughed and Miranda said "She's not joking. My dad will squeeze a penny into a copper wire. He is that tight fisted with money. Well maybe not that bad but he is cheaper than mom."

Al said "I'm sure going to miss you girls always making people laugh with your cute phrases.

Ebony said "No talk of anyone leaving tonight. We only want happy talk. It has been a great year and we have made some of the best friends anyone could ask for. I love you all." Everyone chimed in with "We love you too." "So everybody lift your glasses to friends for life. We will always and forever be The Love Club." They all made the cheer and finished out the night dancing and talking. But mainly just enjoying each other's company.

When the night was over and Mariah and Miranda were in bed that night they could not sleep for reliving every second of the prom. Every word their friends had said. They just didn't want to let go of it.

Not yet anyway. It was the most glamorous night of their life and they were still in a dream stage they didn't want to wake up from ever.

The next couple of weeks all the seniors were getting ready for graduation and the other classes were busy taking end of year test. Before you knew it the last day of school was upon them. They were all heading onto a new grade next year or off to another phase of their life. But one thing was for sure they would always be friends and they promised to stay in touch.

Chris and Miranda, Jaylin and Mariah still had a summer to go through together. They were looking forward to that. Of course they would have everyone else over during the summer to swim so they knew where all the ones staying would be during the summer. The Love club had brought them real love. A great boyfriend and great friends. What would next year bring?

About the time they were wondering this Aniya came running toward them all excited. "Guess what everyone?

Coach Drake ask my mom to marry him and she said yes. She said we could all be in the wedding in November." "Well Mariah said I guess it was called the love club for a reason. Everyone profits when love is involved." Then they all ran to the gym to congratulate Coach Drake and Sam. Next time they ran down these halls they would be sophomores.

TO BE CONTINUED!

ABOUT THE AUTHOR

Donna Faulkner Schulte was born in Fayetteville, North Carolina. She liked writing poems and stories at an early age. She loved to read and would read a book in a couple of hours. Her favorite authors were Stephen King and Dean Koonce. Her other hobbies were music and singing.

She always had the imagination and desire to write about things that happened when she was a child. She likes to use her books to get children to thinking about how to treat others. These things were always a part of her life as shown to her by her parents. Both spent their whole life helping others.

Donna is married and has 3 daughters and 8 grand children and 2 great grandsons. Making up poems and stories for them is what caused her to start writing. She likes to write books about Children and Teens that do good and make changes in the world. It is her hope that her books will inspire these actions to become true with the children that read them. She is a firm believer that one person can make a difference, and wants to instill this in all the youth of the world today. To always believe in yourself and to always hold your hand out to help others.

This will be her second book. Her first book Santa's search for the Perfect Child is also befitting as a life lesson for Children.